IMAGINE!
THOUGHT-PROVOKING POETRY

ACROSS THE PAGE

Edited By Sarah Waterhouse

Queen Mary's College

First published in Great Britain in 2021 by:

Young Writers® Est. 1991

Young Writers
Remus House
Coltsfoot Drive
Peterborough
PE2 9BF
Telephone: 01733 890066
Website: www.youngwriters.co.uk

All Rights Reserved
Book Design by Ashley Janson
© Copyright Contributors 2021
Softback ISBN 978-1-80015-310-3

Printed and bound in the UK by BookPrintingUK
Website: www.bookprintinguk.com
YB0467CZ

FOREWORD

Since 1991, here at Young Writers we have celebrated the awesome power of creative writing, especially in young adults, where it can serve as a vital method of expressing their emotions and views about the world around them. In every poem we see the effort and thought that each pupil published in this book has put into their work and by creating this anthology we hope to encourage them further with the ultimate goal of sparking a life-long love of writing.

Our latest competition for secondary school students, Imagine, challenged young writers to delve into their imaginations to conjure up alternative worlds where anything is possible. We provided a range of speculative questions to inspire them from 'what if kids ruled the world?' to 'what if everyone was equal?' or they were free to use their own ideas. The result is this creative collection of poetry that imagines endless possibilities and explores the consequences both good and bad.

We encourage young writers to express themselves and address subjects that matter to them, which sometimes means writing about sensitive or contentious topics. If you have been affected by any issues raised in this book, details on where to find help can be found at www.youngwriters.co.uk/info/other/contact-lines

CONTENTS

Al-Burhan Grammar School, Tyseley

Fatima Begum (13)	1
Leena Tantawy (12)	2
Reyha Rafiq (13)	4
Sara Iqbal (13)	6
Aisha Navid (12)	7
Minna Ahmed (13)	8
Laiba Munir (12)	9
Zayna Noor (12)	10
Maisha Ahmed (12)	11
Nawal Asim (13)	12
Zara Ali (12)	13
Areebah Rafi (13)	14
Aishah Iqbal (12)	15

Ellesmere Port Catholic High School, Whitby

Callum Potter (15)	16
Bethany Gilfoyle (12)	17
Melody Murphy-Willis (11)	18
Corey Davies (12)	19
Reuben Daniel Geoffrey Owen (14)	20
Katie Jones (11)	21

Iqra Academy, Peterborough

Amina Bi (12)	22
Sidra Rehman (14)	24
Safya Nasiri (14)	25
Malaiqa Khan (13)	26
Marwa Arif Khan (13)	27
Safa Arif Khan (13)	28

Manchester Islamic Grammar School For Girls, Chorlton

Muskaan Shahid (14)	29
Faizah Younus (12)	30
Fatima Sabrah (13)	32
Ayesha Malik (13)	33
Natir Abouzakhar (13)	34
Gezalla Abubaker (12)	35
Areeba Butool (12)	36

Queen Mary's College, Basingstoke

Monty Rice (17)	37
Milanne Deabill (17)	38
Phoebe Purver (18)	40
Felicity Thompson (16)	42
Sinéad Lucas (17)	44
Alice Poynter (16)	46
Alice Johnson (17)	48
Taryn Petzer (17)	49
Charlie Bowden (17)	50
Isobel Thomas (17)	51
Briony Merriman (16)	52
Ryan-James (RJ) Bell (17)	53
Katie Renfrew (19)	54
Rosie Coughlan (17)	55
James Richardson (17)	56
Natascha Buckley (17)	57
Charlie Sargent (18)	58
Anna Johnson (18)	59

South Wigston High School, Wigston

Rachelle Bruce (11)	60
Joshua Mole (11)	62
Thomas Rawlings (11)	63
Emme Briers (11)	64
Archie Hill (11)	65
Olivia Nutter (12)	66
Allisya-Mae Birkin (12)	67
Ashden Jones (12)	68
Ted Wheldale (11)	69
Maddison Merry (12)	70
Katie Green (11)	71
Logan Bennett (11)	72
Kaci-Jae Jones (11)	73
Kirsty Wilson (11)	74
Ruby Baldwin (11)	75
Jamie Ludden (11)	76
Jack Maximus Slater (12)	77

St Philip Howard Catholic High School, Barnham

Hannah Hurst (12)	78
Daisy Jenkins (11)	79
Arkadiusz Wozniak (12)	80
Eryn Chown (12)	81
Marcus Alvarez-Wisby (12)	82

The Thetford Academy, Thetford

Madison Margrie (13)	83
Chloe Louise Gibson (11)	84
Tyler Mark-Conlon (14)	86
Lucy Dimmock (13)	88
Maisy Gibson (11)	89
Taylor Mark-Conlon (14)	90
Maria Zeveolei (13)	91
Sam Brown (13)	92
Alfie Mayhew (13)	93
Nathan Bailey (13)	94
Ieva Sakelyte (12)	95
Lexie Devlin (14)	96
Alfie Wood (11)	97
Krystian Huczek (13)	98
Millie Vendy (13)	100
Holly Rose Cooper (13)	101
Laila Webb (14)	102
Olivia Wall (14)	103
Joe Peters (13)	104
Evita Rasplochaite (14)	105
Jaydie-Ann Lamb (13)	106
Vanesa Berzina (12)	107
Kayla Bogacki (14)	108
Lucy Ellis (11)	109
Dylan Odey (14)	110
Faith Pleszko (14)	111
Sarah Soares (13)	112
Sophie Clarke (14)	113
Lily-Mai Brady (12)	114
Tom Peters	115
Amber Way (12)	116
Brontë Manning (12)	117
Rugile Slanciauskaite	118
Jasmine Reyes (12)	119
Patrick Chaves (11)	120
Luciana Nuttel-Cid (12)	121
Lola Winstone (14)	122
Aleksander Nowicki (11)	123
Aaron Harvey (11)	124
Alfie Pittman (11)	125
Nevaeh Azevedo (11)	126
Dylan Higgins Fitzpatrick (11)	127
Fergus Steward (14)	128
Mia Macpherson-Youldon (11)	129
Lilly-Ann O'Connor (11)	130
Tianna Jade Mark-Conlon (12)	131
Thomas Norkett (12)	132
Daniel Bailey-Green (12)	133
Chloe Bowley (11)	134
Keira-Marie Mulligan (13)	135
Molly Sawbridge (12)	136
Jaiden Lowry (11)	137
Sophie Cunningham (12)	138
Elena-Miruna Mincu (14)	139
Nikodem Olszewski (13)	140

Natalie Daly (12)	141
Rosie Higgins (11)	142
Grace Cuff (11)	143
Grace Palmer (12)	144
Summer Finmager (11)	145
TJ Curtis (14)	146
Kia Dodds (14)	147
Jakub Kosciewicz	148
Mason Edmunds (13)	149
Clive Killick (14)	150
Freddie Griffiths (12)	151
Lilly Macro (13)	152
Alfie Dale (13)	153
Elise Conway (13)	154
Samuel Teixeira (12)	155
Megan James (11)	156

THE POEMS

If Dreams Came True...

Imagine if dreams were real,
Just think how that would feel.
You could have anything at all,
You could live in a castle that's really tall.
You could be the queen of all the land,
You could make diamonds out of sand.
You could have all the money in the world
And sit on a throne that is pearled.
You could eat cake for every meal,
Anything you imagine would become real.
You could live in a world of fantasy
And, if you wanted, you could make it a reality.
You could talk to animals or fly like a bird,
Everyone would do what you wanted just with a word.
Imagine everything you could do
If your dreams came true.

Fatima Begum (13)
Al-Burhan Grammar School, Tyseley

Imagine Fifty Years Down The Road

Imagine fifty years down the road,
Where little children are seated in a classroom.
They look eagerly upon their history teacher,
Awaiting their latest history lesson.
They ponder about their previous classes,
About gruesome and vicious civil wars.
But what comes next is completely unexpected,
For they hear about a world as dramatic as a movie.

They listen, awestruck, about a time,
Where people were stuck at home with school online,
Thousands died every day
And families were kept far, far apart
Suffering pursued till a vaccine was found,
But irreversible damage had been done.

The little children rush home,
To their grandparents' warm, comforting embrace,
And sob out the terrifying image, with large pitiful eyes,
Pictured in their sympathetic, innocent minds.
Their grandparents listen so intently
And sigh, with amused smiles on their faces.

Grandma says, "All I remember was Mother
Teaching me how to bake,

And playing gamecards with siblings all day."
Grandpa recalls, "That's when I learnt
To play football in our back garden."
"We made such memories in the hard times
And always looked on the bright side."
"My dear darlings, from this we can learn
To make the best of our situations."
"For those were the best years of our long lives,
Whilst others looked at what they did not have."
This world is all about perspective,
See it right and it will be bliss and paradise.

Leena Tantawy (12)
Al-Burhan Grammar School, Tyseley

Imagine... Miseries Of The War!

Imagine if you were them,
Bombs dropping in the distance,
People crying for assistance,
Buildings shattered,
Corpses scattered,
Dust filling the air,
My ears stunned as the sirens blare.

Imagine if you were them,
Your world sorrowful and grey,
People going blindly astray,
They can no longer fight,
Holding each other tight,
As trains release a long breath,
Children knowing each step leads to death,
Standing there to be taken,
Hearts where no hope may awaken.

Imagine if you were them,
In pain,
Nothing to gain,
Nazis upping their game,
Leaving everything in one big flame,

Hoping everything would be left the same,
Giving England its victory name.

Imagine if you were them,
As the war came to an end,
No need to fend,
Cheers filling the street,
Enough food to eat,
Smiles spread across,
People pitying whom they lost.

Fear left many souls,
We've achieved our goals.
Imagine...

Reyha Rafiq (13)
Al-Burhan Grammar School, Tyseley

Imagine If?

Imagine if you could change history
Imagine if you could go back in time

Imagine going back to Stone Age times
Or to meet Abraham Lincoln once or twice

Fix all the problems between England and Germany
While having an ally ceremony

To stop the racism between Islam and Christianity
And to gain humanity for all

The endangered lives of all in the tower on the day of 9/11
Who knew that would have happened on the 11th?
Imagine if we could change history
Imagine if we could go back in time
The world can be a horrible place
But we can make it right.

Sara Iqbal (13)
Al-Burhan Grammar School, Tyseley

Imagine If They Knew The Real You

The tears, the hardships I have faced
They are lucky to be so graced

Inside me is a monster so evil
I could never be so civil
I've never felt treasured
Because of the pain I have endured

If they knew who I am, they'd set me under lock and key
Where I would never be free
My life would twist and turn
Making my stomach churn

I've never been glued to a space
Instead, I've been moved place to place
I've never made any friends
I suppose this will never end
Imagine if they knew the real me.

Aisha Navid (12)
Al-Burhan Grammar School, Tyseley

Imagine If They Knew The Pain

Imagine if they knew how much pain
Goes on inside my brain,
The laughter, the mockery,
The ridiculing and trickery,
How deep their words cut me
And they would never feel sorry,
Day after day,
My world stays grey.

Imagine if they saw inside
And realised how much I cry,
Not that they would care,
My life remains unfair,
I am quiet and shy,
But they are rude and sly,
My life is a nightmare
And a frightful scare.

Imagine if they knew how much pain,
Every day, I am emotionally slain.

Minna Ahmed (13)
Al-Burhan Grammar School, Tyseley

Imagine If Kids Ruled The World...

There would be no rules,
There would be chaos all around,
Parents would be on the ground
Saying,
"Oh, what's going on?"
"Everything will be gone!"
Children cheering with glee,
Others on their knees,
Chocolate and sweets for dinners,
Kids would be the winners,
Staying up in the night,
Whilst sleeping in the light,
Watching TV all day,
On the sofa, they would lay,
No more books,
Focusing on looks,
Hiding in their dens,
Writing with pens,
Freedom, freedom, freedom.

Laiba Munir (12)
Al-Burhan Grammar School, Tyseley

Imagine That Was You

Imagine if they knew what happened to you,
They would never want to be in your shoes,
Life is such a mystery
Her story will go down in history.

They thought nothing much
She went inside her closet and hoped she remained untouched.
She ran on her way to school
But every time she came home, she still remained abused.

Her teachers noticed she was down
On her face it showed, she had a frown,
Home was not her happy place,
She gazed outside as she wanted to run away...

Zayna Noor (12)
Al-Burhan Grammar School, Tyseley

Imagine If The World Would End

Imagine if the world would end
Nothing would be able to mend,
The world would become silent
And the wind would become violent...

The children cried
While the parents lied,
The world was dark,
There was no trace of a mark

The wind hustled
While the trees rustled,
The buildings fell,
It was like an image of Hell.

They knew the end had come
Everyone felt numb,
They knew it was the date
To see their fate.

Maisha Ahmed (12)
Al-Burhan Grammar School, Tyseley

Imagine If The World Stopped Spinning...

Imagine if the world stopped spinning,
Everyone would regret their sinning.

Some stuck in eternal light,
While others are stuck in eternal night.

The end of the human race is near,
People are all stricken with regret and fear.

Everyone knows the Earth isn't here for an eternity,
Yet nobody accepts the reality.

Gone with the wind,
How could anyone be so blind,
How could this never cross your mind?

Nawal Asim (13)
Al-Burhan Grammar School, Tyseley

Imagine If Everyone Was Filled With Pain

Imagine if everyone was filled with pain
Everything would be so plain.

Everyone's anger building up inside
People would want to hide.

Violence would fill the streets
Everyone would be scared to meet.

Life would be filled with sorrow
Everyone would be so hollow.

The sky would stay grey
Nothing would ever be the same.

We're all in pain
When will we ever be happy again?

Zara Ali (12)
Al-Burhan Grammar School, Tyseley

Imagine If I Were Them...

Imagine if I were them
Finding food to help me survive

I would be a criminal in disguise

The world would be extremely different
Asking for money whilst I
Sit there on the streets

Thinking if my life would ever change as I
Sit there begging for help.
If only someone could help
Everyone walking around carelessly
Me thinking about how my life could
Work differently.

Areebah Rafi (13)
Al-Burhan Grammar School, Tyseley

Imagine If The World Was About To End...

Dead bodies on the ground
And some yet to be found

Lightning bolts in the sky
And birds flapping to fly

Finding somewhere to hide
While buildings collapse at your side

Horrid things cross your sight
And now it's dark, no more light

The world is on fire
And no one can save it
It's all over
The world is about to end...

Aishah Iqbal (12)
Al-Burhan Grammar School, Tyseley

Imagine

Imagine a world where we are equal,
Imagine a world where we can see past skin colour,
Imagine a world where sexuality doesn't matter,
Imagine a world where cops don't murder innocent people,
Imagine a world where religion isn't ashamed,
Imagine a world where we aren't a hateful species,
Imagine we didn't shame others for fame and money,
Imagine a world where we celebrate differences,
Imagine a world where we haven't turned sour.

Change starts with you.
Imagine a world future generations could be proud of.
Imagine.

Callum Potter (15)
Ellesmere Port Catholic High School, Whitby

Imagine If We Were Them...

Imagine if we were in the 2D world,
Knowing our existence was to please those we didn't know

Imagine if we were in a horror game,
Knowing any second could be our death

Imagine if we were avatars in a video game,
Knowing our lives were on repeat

Imagine if our life was a perfect dream,
Knowing if we woke up, some terror could await us

Imagine if our nightmares were real,
Knowing we could lose so much good that we had

What if that is the case,
What if we are living in those realities unknowingly?

Bethany Gilfoyle (12)
Ellesmere Port Catholic High School, Whitby

Imagine If Your Fears Came True

Imagine if your fears came true
How would you cope and what would you do?

The fears that haunted you for years
And made all those tears.

Every night, you climbed in bed
Those fears came back in your head.

You would scream for your mum or dad
But there was nothing they could do to get rid of the bad.

Paranoid and scared, you would open your eyes
And soon realise
There was no good left in the skies.

Eventually, you would get to sleep
And those dreams would come back like they were on repeat.

Melody Murphy-Willis (11)
Ellesmere Port Catholic High School, Whitby

The World Is About To End

If the world was about to end, what would you do?
Would you spend time with family?
Would you go on holiday?
Could you run away and not look back?
Could you look back through all the memories and all the good things you had?
Should you go and fix what is wrong?
Should you make it all right?
Shall you go and say sorry for what isn't right?
Shall you make friends will all those who are enemies?

If the world was about to end, what would you do?

Corey Davies (12)
Ellesmere Port Catholic High School, Whitby

Imagine Her

Imagine if she was here
Imagine if she hadn't left
Imagine if I could say goodbye
Imagine if I could give back the ring I kept.

But, in reality, she is gone
But, in reality, the memories of her remain
And my love for her will never wane.

"I wish not for sadness," she would say,
"Be joyous on this most sunny day."

Reuben Daniel Geoffrey Owen (14)
Ellesmere Port Catholic High School, Whitby

Imagine If Dinosaurs Were Still Here!

Imagine if dinosaurs were still here!
You would hear them getting nearer and nearer
As they stomp around
Looking for prey,
You better hope that you are safe.
You could ride around on them
All day straight,
But you would have to make sure
That you don't become what they ate!

Katie Jones (11)
Ellesmere Port Catholic High School, Whitby

Imagine If Dreams Could Come True...

Imagine...
One day, everyone's dreams came true...
Just think, whatever we wished for came true...
All magically came true...
Imagine!

How would you feel
If you wished for a million pounds
If you wished for an enormous mansion
If you wished for an iPad, PS5 or even an iPhone 11?
Imagine you got them all...
Just imagine, imagine, imagine!

Just think for a moment, your friends seeing you with designer things
Just imagine complete strangers wanting to be your friend
Just imagine walking, talking and spending time with famous people
Just imagine no schools

If dreams could come true
I would imagine being rich, famous and having everything in the world.
If dreams could come true
I would imagine

I do imagine and
I will continue to imagine!

Amina Bi (12)
Iqra Academy, Peterborough

Imagine If...

Imagine if everyone was equal
Leaders of the world wouldn't divide us into two
I see it and you see it too
How the world divides us in two
There would be no black and no white
There would be no high and no low
We're all human after all
Imagine no more petty distinction of rank and class
Let's all just be friends, at last
Peace is kindness and kindness is to care
Peace is sharing, not evil and spite
Imagine equality and fairness were the essences of peace
Now equality lets us become virtues
Peaceful indeed with those who surround us
And pass on this joy to those full of greed
And make wonderful memories to cherish and share
Imagine if everyone was equal.

Sidra Rehman (14)
Iqra Academy, Peterborough

Imagine If You Could Change History

Imagine one day you open your eyes
And everyone is counting on you,
You hear words of praises and cheers,
All you hear is, "You can do it!"
These thoughts keep on repeating in your head again and again.

Imagine everybody's future depends on your decision,
That one decision you make can be a matter of life and death,
That one word you say can end everything,
Everyone depending on that little hope they have.

Imagine these thousands and thousands of people,
Grandparents, parents, daughters, sons, sisters and brothers,
All those people looking up to you,
You could be the role model of all those people.
Imagine if you could change history!

Safya Nasiri (14)
Iqra Academy, Peterborough

If Humans Never Existed

If humans never existed...
Would the world be twisted?
Would animals be gifted?
Or would they be ballistic?

Would the animals act humanlike?
Would some be able to ride a bike?
Or maybe go on a hike?
Or start a war with an air strike?

Would animals discriminate others?
Would there be different cultures
Of fur, gills and feathers?
Would they enjoy summer?

Or would they still be normal?
Would fish stay by the coral?
Would some stay nocturnal?
Would they still have quarrels?

Malaiqa Khan (13)
Iqra Academy, Peterborough

Imagine

Imagine we were all identical,
No one would know who's who,
No one would know who their friend was,
Everyone would be confused,
Life would be hard!

Imagine we were all identical,
We all wore the same clothes,
We had the exact same features.

Imagine we were all identical,
We were the same age,
Same birthday,
Same height,
Same weight,
It would be a confusing world!

Imagine...

Marwa Arif Khan (13)
Iqra Academy, Peterborough

Imagine If We All Spoke The Same Language...

We would all understand each other
There would be no misunderstandings
We would all share the same language

Everything would be written in the same language
It would be the one and only language in the world
There would be no language lessons

We would not be judged for speaking the language
The world would be more efficient
We'd all be similar in some way.

Safa Arif Khan (13)
Iqra Academy, Peterborough

My Perfect World

Imagine we were in a world where nobody cared about black or white,
Imagine being in a world where racism wasn't heard or in sight,
Imagine being in a world where everyone got along,
Imagine being in a world where life was like a lovely song,
Imagine being in a world where spiders turned into flowers,
Imagine being in a world where we all had magical powers,
Imagine feeling so elated that sad wasn't a feeling anymore,
Imagine being in a world where we all danced in joy galore,
Imagine being in a world where happiness filled the sky,
Imagine being in a world so good it wasn't a lie,
Imagine being in a world without terror or fear,
Imagine being in a world without a sorrowful tear,
Wouldn't that be a perfect world where the despondent sea creatures would see light?
Or when countries would make up from their fight?
And when the Earth begins to breathe again?
What a world!

Muskaan Shahid (14)
Manchester Islamic Grammar School For Girls, Chorlton

Imagine

Imagine if everyone was equal,
No one is different,
All treated the same,
A place where no one is alone.

Imagine if everyone was equal,
No one alone,
The world whole, as one,
Together we stand.

Imagine if everyone was equal,
No one standing alone,
All standing united, as one.

Imagine if everyone was equal,
The world would be different,
The world would be boring,
A world where no one is unique,
A world no one can call their own,
But a place where we are all equal.

Imagine if everyone was equal,
No man, no woman, no child... different,
All the same,
All treated the same,
Looked after the same,
A home, a road, a neighbourhood,

A village, a town, a city, a country,
The world
We are all equal...
Anywhere.

Faizah Younus (12)
Manchester Islamic Grammar School For Girls, Chorlton

Imagine If...

Imagine if you stopped wearing yourself out,
You stopped tearing yourself apart to entertain,
You stopped belittling yourself in the bringing up of others,
Day by day,
The happy child you used to be shields away,
A gradual yet sure fate.
What is wrong with you?
How did this begin?
Your friends suppose.
Constantly pointing out your insecurities
And blowing it off as a cold 'joke',
A snowflake you are
Words cutting deeper each day over and over,
Bashing yourself over and over,
Losing joy in the things you loved doing.
A hopeless pit you're stuck in,
Feeling this way is stupid?
No.
Hurting someone emotionally to the point of feeling this way is stupid.
No one will ever love you like I do.

Fatima Sabrah (13)
Manchester Islamic Grammar School For Girls, Chorlton

Imagine

Imagine if the voices in my head got along with me
Imagine if a smile could get rid of all our worries
Imagine if I could be accepted for just being me
Imagine if everyone was equal
Imagine if there was no sadness or pain
Imagine if there were no wars
Imagine if no one cared about my looks, only about my personality
Imagine if there was no racism
Imagine if there was only peace
Imagine if society loved everyone
Imagine if there was no terrorism
Imagine if people who changed the world could see the changes in the world

I have a dream,
A dream that someday
My imagination could become reality

Just imagine,
It could happen.

Ayesha Malik (13)
Manchester Islamic Grammar School For Girls, Chorlton

Imagine

Imagine if you could see the future
Imagine what you would be
Who you would be
What you would be capable of
Imagine
If you were rich or poor
Content or discontent
Angry or sensitive
Imagine what technology would be like
What people would be like, what their personalities would be like
What your status would be
If the world was at peace and with prosperity
No war, no death, no rules, no nothing
Imagine if people knew how to spend money wisely
How rich the economy would be
How many loved ones died
How many animals died
Just imagine.

Natir Abouzakhar (13)
Manchester Islamic Grammar School For Girls, Chorlton

Imagine

Imagine if you could fly...
Imagine if everyone was equal
Imagine if you could see the future

Just imagine!

Imagine if you could change the weather...
Imagine if there were no fires and no climate change
Never!
Imagine if buildings were as light as a feather

Just imagine!

Life is perfect, like a peacock feather
Even though it's tethered.

Gezalla Abubaker (12)
Manchester Islamic Grammar School For Girls, Chorlton

Imagine If

Imagine if the world was about to end
And you were the only one left;
There wouldn't be anyone else except you,
Not your family, not your friends,
"Only you! No one else."
Volcanoes exploding and rushing towards my house,
Me running here and there
And buildings crushed, nowhere to go.
Imagine if the world was about to end,
No one left.

Areeba Butool (12)
Manchester Islamic Grammar School For Girls, Chorlton

Grief

You will feel this blessing for as long as your heart needs it;
the larger the heart, the longer it takes to heal.
Wear your scars for they make you; they are you,
they make you brighter than without them.

Go forward and cry on the shoulder of your enemy,
for they have parallels with yourself.
In your meditated state of anger, you shall peer into the eye that peeks behind glass,
to realise there is no hate, but willingness to love each other.

Lost in the sandpits of the children's playground,
you will reclaim this spirit with reward.
Then you can stand by each other and finally be able to speak:
"We are of the same foundation, built up without care,
but connected on the ground we pray on."

Monty Rice (17)
Queen Mary's College, Basingstoke

Imagine A World...

Imagine if I could write a salve
And everything could be solved,
Every wrong would just dissolve,
Could we do it, could we evolve?

Imagine no one dead or dying because of their skin,
People not thinking that other skins are sins,
Instead, judging someone's character and what's within
And the war against racism was one we'd finally win.

Imagine somewhere no one thought, *it'd be better if I were gone,*
I just really wish I'd never been born
And that the 2019 suicide statistic for England alone
Wasn't high at five thousand, six hundred and ninety-one.

Imagine if we lived in a world that wasn't dying
And nobody was in doubt or denying,
Where oceans stayed and ice caps and forests weren't frying,
Somewhere, Mother Nature wasn't constantly crying.

Imagine a world where people had what they needed already,
No one would be begging on the street for just a penny
And every hungry child had food aplenty,
Where the needs of the few were equal to the needs of those who have many.

Imagine if people were free to love who they wished
And victims of hate crimes didn't need to be missed,
Because LGBTQ+ people could just exist
Without anyone getting their knickers in a twist.

Imagine a place nobody was hurt gratuitously
And people weren't dying far too suddenly,
Because someone wanted to 'get them' maliciously,
Somewhere unwarranted violence didn't happen numerously.

But I don't think a salve would work or last,
Nothing could be saved how I asked,
Each wrong stays and probably won't pass,
It seems we can't evolve, in contrast.

Milanne Deabill (17)
Queen Mary's College, Basingstoke

Not An Attack, Just A Plea

Imagine our world was dying,
Sizzling, sweltering, suffocating
from clean air.
The pungent, sticky, icky breath of wealth,
adds coal to the burning fire,
determined to keep their pockets full
with dirt and minerals they scrape from the barrel of our rich earth.
Hungry: to be more deceitful
fills their bellies every night
as they munch on their lies to help change.

Imagine our world is dying.
Screams of species
shall choke and froth
in a pile of their own oozing last gasp,
which clearly boils up heaps of cash
for the people on their chairs so high.
Let us skin humans alive next
for it keeps them rich and the globe divided.
Pushing the homeless to groundless
is the modern form of patriotism.
Leaving desperate souls in terror.

Our world is dying.
Listen to the screams of our planet and people,
the world will melt your precious money with it.

For the crudity of your priorities
denies life its potential
and satisfies the same genre of negligence.
We are begging for the power you own,
use it to fuel the fresh inhale of a healthy globe,
provide a path for lives which have been stripped.
Or your temporary flood gates will burst with a last sigh.
Please, please, please,
help us to help you to not let our world die.

Phoebe Purver (18)
Queen Mary's College, Basingstoke

Grounding My Monster

There was a monster under my bed,
My monster is quite scary
My mummy says what's under the bed
Is just imaginary

But what I haven't told my mummy,
The thing she doesn't know,
My monster moved to the very place
I asked it not to go

My hair became the bird's nest
In which my monster sleeps
And though they rent, they make me pay
And, trust me, rent's not cheap.

It finds a home for its bags,
Stored underneath my eyes,
While I just pray the downpour
Won't expose what hides inside.

My feet trail along the tiled floor,
Tied down by paper chains,
Some days, I can't move from my bed -
Those are the days it rains.

It keeps its sugar in my veins
As I struggle to relax,

Hyper-aware, sweating, shaking,
Just waiting to be attacked

And though I say I'm okay
When my friends ask if I'm fine,
I see their monster hiding too,
Behind their haunted eyes.

I was told to tell my mother
The thing she didn't know,
About the thoughts my monster makes -
She just asked me to go.

I miss when my monster was under my bed,
I miss that way it scared me,
I miss when the thing that was under my bed
Was just imaginary.

Felicity Thompson (16)
Queen Mary's College, Basingstoke

Close Your Eyes

Close your eyes
And imagine a world of you and me,
Nothing left but the two of us.
The world is silent, the world has stopped.
In this world of quiet, we don't just survive,
We live.

The world's a stage and we its players,
Dancing, singing, round and round
'Make them laugh,
Make them cry,
Elicit some emotion'.
All the while,
The world passing by.

We rule the world,
Bring cities to their knees,
Queens with robes flowing in the breeze.
We reign,
Your compassion counteracting my iron fist.
We are feared and loved,
Held in awe and esteem,
But all that matters is the two of us.

We're alone, just us,
Just you and I.
Sun streams through the leaves

In our little glade.
The grass is soft,
The wind a caress,
We lie down,
Hold each other
And fade.

The world moves on
And we go with it.
The days pass by,
The chasm narrows,
You are closer than you have ever been.
One day, my love,
You'll be here with me.
But for now,
Just close your eyes,
Imagine,
And think of me.

Sinéad Lucas (17)
Queen Mary's College, Basingstoke

Fragmented Dreams

Fragmented dreams of broken hope
Scratching through the walls to cope
Lay their roots to touch a lost thought
Breaking what I've been taught

Sitting in this empty room
Building my very own tomb
Waiting for the day to come
When this room fills with sun

Still lost within fragmented dreams
Broken hope ripples upon stream
Following these familiar walls
Never diverting from these halls

I step outside my empty room
To be greeted with nought but gloom
I back into my comforting nest
Until my eternal rest

But alas, my safe walls have gone
Leaving me to face what I have done
But dreams are no longer broken
And my hope has not been stolen

I look around my new empty room
Leaving me as I was in unending doom

The gift of unfragmented dreams
Pulled away like reeds in streams

The memories of an old room
Fade away with my doom
Now I know nothing but these empty walls
I no longer remember anything but these halls.

Alice Poynter (16)
Queen Mary's College, Basingstoke

Imagine

Imagine your life is the universe:
If your tears are the waves, then you are the ocean
If your struggles are the storms, then you are the sky
If your feelings are the planets, then you are the solar system
If your insecurities are the stars, then you are the galaxy
You are more than the weather -
You are not your cloudy thoughts, you are clouded by your thoughts
You are not the storm, you go *through* the storm
And sometimes you just have to let it rain, let your tears flow, and that's okay.
Because even if light is not in sight,
The sun will be there, shining bright...

Life is always worth the fight,
No matter how dark it may seem tonight.

Alice Johnson (17)
Queen Mary's College, Basingstoke

Nearly Senseless

When I close my eyes
I fit my soles in your shoes
And imagine that once my eyes reopen
We'll be sharing the same view

But we're in different seasons
The sky is now cold to me
While, for you, it thunders
So loud, yet not heard across the sea

If my thoughts had power
Our left hands would be intertwined
I'd be your wrapped-in-love present
And your presence would be mine

But our hands are clasped only in memory
Your touch is gone
Your scent forgotten
Your smile fading
I should just try to listen
For the echoes of the thunder.

Taryn Petzer (17)
Queen Mary's College, Basingstoke

In Your Image

You are god of nothing, citizen of nowhere,
A tried-and-true false prophet.
Hope is your citadel, intention your usher.
Weave milk and honey on your loom of broken ribs,
Earth shall be decadent in the shrieks of seraphim.
How weary the silken womb of your mind will be.

The heart of the dust becomes a pulse so bright,
Shatter the glass, transform the spectral starlight.
Balled fists, blind faith, white-hot belief,
Orgies of galaxies fashioned in brief.
Rent tranquillity for the children of Judea
Nothing stops you - you are nothing but an idea.

Charlie Bowden (17)
Queen Mary's College, Basingstoke

Canvas

My eyes invade colours - navy blue,
From camo greens to scarlet platoon.
From Artillery Fire that ignites the sky
Fireworks ablaze bring impending doom.

Richard of York gave battle in vain,
So veins stain scarlet that pure white snow.
Wildflower poppies bloom from below
To scatter the grounds like fallen men.

My eyes evade bodies painted black and blue,
Evade gruesome bruises green and red blood too.
The young and old - all embossed with colour.
A bloody rainbow -
Too much to muster
All gaze upon the dismal view.

Isobel Thomas (17)
Queen Mary's College, Basingstoke

Clay

A little clay figurine
In the calloused hand of whoever -
The fingerprint of your best friend
Into your chest.

More clay -
She grows.
Keep her changing.
The face is made and set early on -
Keep adding to the limbs,
She gets stronger.

The little clay figurine -
You know the one -
Eyes fixed from across the workshop.
And although the eyes are yours
And you can remember each and every smudge and smooth in its face -
The emotion within them is something you cannot name.

Briony Merriman (16)
Queen Mary's College, Basingstoke

Revenge

Rival, the master, sensed his apprentice.
Embrace the dark side of the force.
Violence is never the answer.
Negativity will cost you freedom.
Gain knowledge and power.
Eyes and body language can be deceiving.

Ryan-James (RJ) Bell (17)
Queen Mary's College, Basingstoke

Christmas

Bright magical elves being kind
Cold crackers unwrapping
Shopping, mouths watering, sparkling angels
Festive Christmassy season celebration
Colourful, families believing
Singing peaceful, exciting songs.

Katie Renfrew (19)
Queen Mary's College, Basingstoke

Grandma

Special, funny Grandma visiting
Kind lady walking
Hugging, caring, lovely family.
Visiting Grandma in hospital
Seeing Grandma at our house
Enjoying having Grandad over for dinner.

Rosie Coughlan (17)
Queen Mary's College, Basingstoke

Christmas
A haiku

Green tree decorate
Shiny lights, wrapping, giving
The exciting presents.

James Richardson (17)
Queen Mary's College, Basingstoke

Christmas

A haiku

Colourful Christmas
Singing, walking, exciting
Christmas tree sparkling.

Natascha Buckley (17)
Queen Mary's College, Basingstoke

Christmas
A haiku

Exciting presents
Festive stockings are hanging
Singing Christmas songs.

Charlie Sargent (18)
Queen Mary's College, Basingstoke

Christmas

A haiku

Christmas tree festive
Joyous is baby Jesus
Sing magical songs.

Anna Johnson (18)
Queen Mary's College, Basingstoke

The Time Travel Machine Mystery

I woke up, it must have been a dream
Because there's no way I can travel through time
There is no way I could see:
Henry VIII beheading Anne Boleyn,
There is no way I could see past people sin
Or kings being killed,
The Victorian era and the Queen being crowned.

I got dressed and saw a time travel machine
OMG, it must have been real, the dream
There were 2020 buttons with years on
I clicked the year '1538'
I appeared in Henry VIII's palace
It was very grand and I saw Henry VIII
I walked right in front of him
Yet he couldn't see me.

I went back in the time machine
And clicked '2015'
The year my grandma died in a car crash
I rushed to her house
And persuaded her to stay at home
I clicked '2020'

My grandma was sitting in my living room with my mum. That's my story of the time travel machine.

Rachelle Bruce (11)
South Wigston High School, Wigston

Imagine

Imagine if I saw Santa!
Imagine if he saw me awake.
Just... imagine
Imagine if I saw an elf
Imagine if I saw an elf on the shelf move. It would be crazy, weird, impossible, berserk!
Imagine if I saw the reindeer! Maybe Rudolph, Blitzen or Comet
Imagine if you had a snowman that could move or get into a snowball fight with you!
Imagine if you were Santa or his helper elf, or imagine if you were his *best* elf.
Imagine if you saw the reindeer fly on Santa's sleigh!
Imagine if your whole town saw him go, "Ho, ho, ho!"
Imagine if you were in his sleigh while it was flying.
Imagine if you were at the North Pole.
Imagine if you saw Santa's workshop and all of the elves working.
Imagine if you saw Santa making a toy.
Imagine if Christmas was every day!

Joshua Mole (11)
South Wigston High School, Wigston

Imagine If You Had One Wish

Imagine if you had one wish,
What would you spend it on?
Would you wish to meet the Queen,
Or would you wish to be the best the world has ever seen?
Would you wish to be immortal,
Would you wish for everyone to be equal,
Would you wish to win the lottery,
Or would you wish for life to be gleeful?
Would you wish to be a superhero,
Would you wish to be in a computer game,
Would you wish to be invisible,
Or would you wish for lots of fame?
Would you wish to rule the world,
Would you wish for a white Christmas,
Would you wish to read people's minds,
Or would you wish to be worryless?

Thomas Rawlings (11)
South Wigston High School, Wigston

End Of The World!

Imagine if the world was about to end,
Say goodbye to all your friends.

Imagine if the ground began to shake,
But it was worse than an earthquake.

Imagine if the buildings crumbled to the ground,
That's all you could see around.

Imagine if you didn't feel safe,
You wouldn't even be able to pack your case.

Imagine if all your loved ones were gone,
It would be like the sun never shone.

Imagine if the uproarious noise suddenly stopped,
You felt yourself about to drop.

Imagine if the world was about to end.

Emme Briers (11)
South Wigston High School, Wigston

Imagine If

Imagine if you were rich,
Imagine if you were poor,
Imagine if you lived in a mansion,
Imagine if you didn't have a house.

Imagine if you lived underwater,
Imagine if you lived in the sky,
Imagine if we lived in the past,
Imagine if we lived in the future.

Imagine if you met the Queen,
Imagine if you met the king.
Imagine if you saw a dinosaur,
Imagine if you saw a megalodon.

Imagine if...

Archie Hill (11)
South Wigston High School, Wigston

Imagine

Imagine if there was no hate in the world,
Just how happy our world would be.

Imagine if everyone was treated equally,
Just how fair this world would be.

Imagine if there was no litter on the streets,
Just how happy the sealife would be.

Imagine if there were no crimes in the world,
Just how safe this world would be.

Imagine if everyone was exactly the same,
Just how boring this world would be.

Olivia Nutter (12)
South Wigston High School, Wigston

Imagine Pets Could Talk

Imagine pets could talk,
But they couldn't walk.
That would be crazy,
Not very many pets are lazy.
Imagine pets could fly,
We hope they never die!
Imagine they could cook
Whilst reading a book.
What if they tidied up?
Go and have a look
Imagine they had feelings
That randomly floated to the ceiling.
What if pets went dancing?
You would only see them prancing.

Allisya-Mae Birkin (12)
South Wigston High School, Wigston

Imagine If You Won The Lottery

Imagine if you won the lottery and you were the wealthiest person in the world.
Imagine if you bought a huge mansion and it had five swimming pools.
Imagine if you owned five companies and you were a billionaire.
Imagine if you had a gold Lamborghini.
Imagine if you were the most famous person there had ever been.
Imagine if you were the CEO of the world bank.
Imagine if you owned a whole country.

Ashden Jones (12)
South Wigston High School, Wigston

Kids Rule

I magine if kids ruled the world,
M illions of McDonald's,
A pples forgotten,
G reat giraffes in our gardens.
I magine if kids ruled the world,
N othing would be boring,
E ating chocolate wouldn't be naughty.

I magine if kids ruled the world,
F orgotten are the rules of the adults.

Ted Wheldale (11)
South Wigston High School, Wigston

My Best Friend

Once, every week, I go round my best friend's house,
And when she leaves for a sec, I am as quiet as a mouse.
I thought it was a good idea to have a look around
And you wouldn't believe what I found.

There was fake skin on the floor,
Suddenly, I heard a creak from her door,
Oh my, she was from outer space!
I need to leave this place...

Maddison Merry (12)
South Wigston High School, Wigston

Imagine If You Were Invisible

Imagine if you were invisible,
Imagine if you could see someone without them knowing,
Imagine if things weren't real,
Imagine if seals weren't animals,
Imagine if you didn't have fears,
Imagine if the universe wasn't real,
Imagine if you were someone else,
Imagine if someone else was you,
Imagine if you were invisible.

Katie Green (11)
South Wigston High School, Wigston

Imagine If Kids Ruled The World

Imagine if kids ruled the world
The girls would be riding unicorns,
The boys would be playing football,
There would be no schools,
We would all be in swimming pools.

All the food would be free
We would all be playing on the Wii,
We would all be driving F1 cars,
We would all have our own bars.

Logan Bennett (11)
South Wigston High School, Wigston

Imagine If You Could See What People Were Thinking

Imagine if you could see what people were thinking,
Imagine if they were thinking about you,
Could be anything,
Evil or nice,
Embarrassing or confusing,
How would you approach them?
Would you tell them you knew?
Don't be scared to tell them,
Make them feel how you felt.

Kaci-Jae Jones (11)
South Wigston High School, Wigston

Imagine

Imagine they knew the real you!
Imagine people could see what you were thinking.
Imagine they *were* you!
Imagine if you could see your future.
Imagine if humans were extinct!
Imagine the world was about to end.

What would you do?
How would you feel?

Kirsty Wilson (11)
South Wigston High School, Wigston

Imagine!

Imagine if everyone was equal
Imagine that racism was gone
Imagine we all got along
Imagine if I had one wish
I would wish that racism was banished.

Imagine if we were all different
Imagine we treated others equally
Imagine if everyone was equal.

Ruby Baldwin (11)
South Wigston High School, Wigston

If Dinosaurs Weren't Extinct

If dinosaurs weren't extinct
We wouldn't be top of the food chain
And many people would be in pain.
If dinosaurs weren't extinct
We would have some as pets
But we would need bigger vets!

Jamie Ludden (11)
South Wigston High School, Wigston

Imagine!

Imagine if I won the lottery,
I would get some lovely toffees,
I'd buy a car,
After, I would get a real star
I'd want a million-pound mansion,
Then I would get lots of fountains.

Jack Maximus Slater (12)
South Wigston High School, Wigston

Imagine

Imagine if you won the lottery,
Imagine if the world was about to end,
Imagine if you could do pottery,
Imagine if you had the world's best friend.

Imagine if you had one wish,
Imagine if you could both eye wink,
Imagine if you had a massive fish,
Imagine if people could see what you think.

Imagine if we were just avatars in a computer game,
Imagine if we were pink,
Imagine if you changed your name,
Imagine if humans were extinct.

Imagine if you could see the future,
Imagine if dreams were real.

Hannah Hurst (12)
St Philip Howard Catholic High School, Barnham

Imagine

Imagine if the world was about to end...
In the messages people would send,
Saying goodbye to your only friend.

Imagine if the world was about to end...
All the things on which you missed out,
How your life is ending without a doubt.

Imagine if the world was about to end...
All the work you didn't complete,
All the things you now have to delete.

Imagine the world was about to end...
Going to the shops and buying everything there,
Now all you can see is a blurry flare.

Daisy Jenkins (11)
St Philip Howard Catholic High School, Barnham

Imagine The World

Imagine if the world was to end.
Imagine if the world turned blue.
Imagine if the world was to bend.
Imagine if the world turned to glue.

Imagine if the world was a bed.
Imagine if the world was a doll.
Imagine if the world was dead.
Imagine if the world was to fall.

Imagine if the world was a train.
Imagine if the world was a leaf.
Imagine if the world was a brain.
Imagine if the world was a reef.

Imagine if the world was a tin.
Imagine if the world was a pin.

Arkadiusz Wozniak (12)
St Philip Howard Catholic High School, Barnham

Imagine

Imagine if we could change history,
Imagine if we won the lottery,
Why is life such a mystery?
Imagine if we could do pottery.

Imagine if we were just avatars in a game,
Imagine if the world was about to end,
Imagine if we were just pictures in a frame,
Imagine if you had the world's best friend.

Imagine if you only had one wish,
Imagine if you were immortal,
Imagine if we were just a fish on a dish,
Imagine if you could go through a portal.

Eryn Chown (12)
St Philip Howard Catholic High School, Barnham

The Moon

The moon is a spark emitting from a blinking light bulb on an abandoned suburban subway station,
The moon is a white circle on a black chalkboard,
The moon is a glow worm circling around the earth,
The moon is an onion on a black cutting board,
The moon is the Earth's best friend,
The moon is a disco ball in a night club,
The moon is a race car as it drives around the track,
The moon is a whole new world to explore,
The moon is always watching you...

Marcus Alvarez-Wisby (12)
St Philip Howard Catholic High School, Barnham

Depression Awareness

I magine spending every minute realising no one can save you from rock bottom.
M ental breakdown that seems endless and impossible to the uneducated eye.
A ctually thinking that coming to terms with your problems makes them worse rather than better.
G etting the same feeling of sadness and hatred, yet pushing it down far enough, forcing a smile and acting seemingly happy.
I tching to break down but knowing better than not showing how weak or damaged someone can really be.
N eeding the constant feeling of love and appreciation, even though you know that you will never feel proud, ending in spiralling despair.
E yes glazed with fake happiness, holding back a river of secret thoughts and unforgiving tears.

Madison Margrie (13)
The Thetford Academy, Thetford

Save The Animals

When you see the sky and Earth
Do you wonder what on earth
Are roaming the skies?
It's majestic birds tweeting
And soaring the skies
But some are getting shot down for fun
Some are losing their homes
Why would they do that?
Save the animals
Save them
Save the animals
Save them, please.
On the Earth, the bear roams the forest
Protecting itself from predators
The humans are predators
To bears, to wolves
To any animals on the Earth
See what humans are doing to animals?
See what they are doing to the world?
Animals are dying or losing their homes
Or becoming extinct
While we do nothing to protect them
Show the animals some kindness!
Show some love
Sure, some animals kill

But do you know the reason why?
Maybe it's because they lost someone in their family
Or had a bad past
Whatever the reason is
They are just protecting themselves
Just save the animals!
Just save them
They are helpless creatures from the Earth
Just like us.

Chloe Louise Gibson (11)
The Thetford Academy, Thetford

Imagine

What I imagine cannot be seen,
What I imagine cannot be foretold.
A mystery which lurks beneath the surface,
A secret that you will never know.

A world full of peace and equality,
Where everyone is cold.
Where all we need is jollity,
Not where we are controlled.

What I imagine cannot be seen,
What I imagine cannot be foretold.
A barren place with frost and ice,
Somewhere humans cannot find.

A world where everything is dark,
No light will shine upon us.
No one will find our mark,
Unless one of us is possessed.

What I imagine cannot be seen,
What I imagine cannot be foretold.
A desire so strong and rich,
To be shattered once again.

Greed and wealth is not essential,
What matters now is that we survive.

For it will ruin our potential,
A place full of the unalive.

What I imagine cannot be seen,
What I imagine cannot be foretold.
So, take my advice
And you might not get trapped in the underplot.

Tyler Mark-Conlon (14)
The Thetford Academy, Thetford

Imagining

Imagine life tirelessly moving,
Never stopping to really be alive,
Imagine life ever changing,
But always staying the same.

Imagine people living for each other,
Showing how kindness should be,
Imagine people standing together,
Reminding us how to be free.

Imagine believing in yourself,
Pushing your hopes and dreams,
Imagine believing in hope,
Even though times are hard.

Imagine dreaming of happier times,
Smiling widely through memories,
Imagine dreaming of greater things,
Being unstoppable for your own good.

Imagine a world free of illness,
Where loved ones never pass,
Imagine a world free to heal
From festering wounds in the past.

Lucy Dimmock (13)
The Thetford Academy, Thetford

If I Won The Lottery

If I won the lottery
I'd tell you what to do
You'd clean my room
Then you'd walk my dog
And polish my shoes

My slaves would be busy
So leave them alone
Get my dog a golden bone
I'd sit on my throne
While you bow down to your beloved queen

There'd be no rule you'd disobey
No peasant would get in my way
And I'd have more than two slaves
All that I'd want and more

My palace would be clean and gold
Every room would be bright and bold
Silver would be polished
The floors would shine
Look around, this is all mine

Yep! If a welcome windfall came my way,
It's true this is how I'd live every day.

Maisy Gibson (11)
The Thetford Academy, Thetford

What Could Be Seen Was...

Waking up in the dead of night
Only to see a bright light
So, I followed it into the unknown
Into the anticyclone

What happened next could not be foretold
For the future would be uncontrolled
As I stepped away from myself
I truly saw what we desire, ourselves

Looking away from the despair
What I saw would not even compare
For I died straight away
Only to see Heaven's archways

Looking down from up here
All I could see was fear
For what they were, stronger,
They are no longer

Only that that could be seen was seen
But never could it be foreseen.
Stepping away from reality
I finally realised normality.

Taylor Mark-Conlon (14)
The Thetford Academy, Thetford

Just Sit Back And Imagine

Imagine that you are always a stranger
In a world that's not yours, nor was it,
In which others understand each other
In their language! You do not!
It's not your language, and to them
You are forever named a traveller.

Imagine nests without birds
And lakes without fish,
Trees covering the mountains,
When you're not invited to rest
Even though you live there... you do not.
Just sit back and imagine
The world without its beauty.

Imagine a world without colour!
Imagine a world without flowers!
Imagine a world without love
In which I do not want to sneak into,
Then to die...

Maria Zeveolei (13)
The Thetford Academy, Thetford

Imagine If The World Was Ending

Imagine if the world was about to end.
What would you do?
Would it be scary?
How would you react?
Many people would cry,
But others wouldn't believe it...
Would you believe it?
Most people would gather with their friends and families,
Others would stockpile, rob stores,
Make use of the newly unlawed place...
Scary, isn't it?
Most people who are religious would gather in churches and mosques,
Some others wouldn't.
But I think the entire world would go silent,
Only for a few seconds
With the shock of things.
Then the world would turn to havoc.
What would you do?

Sam Brown (13)
The Thetford Academy, Thetford

Imagine A World

Imagine a world of everybody being fit and well
There'd be no more diseases
Nothing to worry about
If everyone was fit and well.

Imagine a world without poverty
Nobody would be sleeping on the streets
Roofs could be put over everybody's heads
If there was a world without poverty.

Imagine a world without government
Nobody to make important country choices
Everything would be a mess
In a world without government.

Imagine a world with super-fast cars
Zooming through the streets at the dead of night
Burning rubber as they go
In the ideal world to live in.

Alfie Mayhew (13)
The Thetford Academy, Thetford

Extraterrestrial Life

I magine if aliens existed
F lying around in their futuristic vehicles

A nd suppose they were watching us
L ike spies watching their targets
I magine what types of weapons they would have
E xtraordinary weapons like no other
N obody would know they were there
S uppose they decided to attack us

E xtraordinary technology we'll never discover
X -ray vision goggles like in the movies
I magine they visited our planet
S aw the damage we have done to it
T hen they turned around and left us forever.

Nathan Bailey (13)
The Thetford Academy, Thetford

Imagine If Everyone Was Nicer...

Imagine if the world was a nicer place,
People wouldn't be killed because of their skin colour.
People wouldn't be upset if everyone accepted their sexuality.
Children would have more friends if other children weren't mean to them.
Teenagers would be pleased about their looks,
If others didn't have hate for their bodies and facial looks.
Adults would stress out less,
Their children nicer and more respectful to them.
Imagine if everyone was nicer,
Everyone would be happy and wouldn't worry about how they look,
What others think
And they could be who they want to be!

Ieva Sakelyte (12)
The Thetford Academy, Thetford

Imagine You Were All Grown Up

Imagine you were all grown up,
Married with kids,
Or a billionaire living alone,
A husband or a wife,
A doctor or a filmmaker,
Ten kids or ten dogs.
Imagine you were all grown up,
Living in a mansion or cottage,
Or an apartment or flat,
Or simply alone in the woods.
You could be married,
Divorced or waiting for the right one,
You may be happy or sad,
Wishing you hadn't grown up so fast,
Or excited you had made it that far.
Imagine you were all grown up,
What do you want it to look like
And how will you get there?
Imagine you were all grown up...

Lexie Devlin (14)
The Thetford Academy, Thetford

If It Wasn't Real

Imagine
Imagine all our knowledge was for nothing
Imagine we were not real
Imagine we were a hologram
Imagine we were pixels floating across the screen
Imagine every time we spoke, it was a text message
Imagine we couldn't speak the truth
Imagine everything was a lie
Imagine we could find the truth
About our existence, the real truth
We must go on to imagine
Then it makes us come together as a team
Find the truth and imagine
Can we imagine forever?
Is there a glitch to the software?
Imagine
Just imagine
Wait until the final moment
And imagine.

Alfie Wood (11)
The Thetford Academy, Thetford

Imagine

Imagine a world
Where nobody cries.
We only need to
When somebody dies.

Imagine a world
Where all love is strong.
Imagine a world
Where no one does wrong.

Imagine a world
Where nobody lies
And everyone loves
Each day they're alive.

Imagine a world
Where there is no war.
Imagine a world
No one serves a tour.

Imagine a world
Where peace rules the streets
And we learn to love
Everyone we meet.

This can be our world,
Only if we try.

We can live in peace,
Or we can choose to die.

Krystian Huczek (13)
The Thetford Academy, Thetford

Imagine If The World Was Yours

Imagine, just imagine
Imagine that the world was yours
Imagine that everything came true
Imagine that everything was under your command
What would you do?

Would you make your dreams come true?
Would you use this ability for the greater good?
But what if this faded away?
Would you imagine it again?
Or would you change it to something better?

How could you make it better?
Imagine that you could fly
Imagine that you could freeze time
Imagine that you were a famous musician
Imagine bright lights surrounding you.

Would you imagine for eternity?

Millie Vendy (13)
The Thetford Academy, Thetford

Imagine

Imagine if everyone wasn't racist,
If everyone was equal,
Imagine if everyone had a bucket list,
If everyone wasn't evil,
Imagine if everyone followed the law
And had no flaws,
Imagine if people weren't homophobic
And people could love who they wanted,
Imagine if people didn't bully
And everyone apologised sincerely,
Imagine if the world was great
And everyone wasn't late,
Imagine if everyone was themselves
And everyone didn't have to change.
You should be you
And not be blue,
Just remember that,
Just imagine that.

Holly Rose Cooper (13)
The Thetford Academy, Thetford

The Bad Dream

I had to pay for that day
When I ran away.
I didn't have a choice
Because no one heard my voice.
I felt alone
Nothing felt like home.

I had to escape
I could not hesitate
This day was the worst
I felt like I was cursed.

I ran as fast as I could
Straight past the woods
Into a dark neighbourhood.

I think I went too far
I ran into a car
All I could see was a big bright star.

I think I hit my head
But I woke up in my bed
I began to scream
Until I realised it was all just a bad dream!

Laila Webb (14)
The Thetford Academy, Thetford

Living A Nightmare

Lying on my bed, I drift off into a state of unawareness.
I wake up and it's a new day.
The day is fresh and the sun is warm.
I start the day as usual and go about like normal.
Something is off.
Everyone seems strange around me,
Some rude, some nice.
I walk away from the shop when I stop at the road.
I walk across, but before I reach the other side,
I am hit by a bus.
I wake up...
Again.
I was having a nightmare.
I brush it off as I start the day.
I soon realise I'm living the exact day as my nightmare.
I might die today.

Olivia Wall (14)
The Thetford Academy, Thetford

Imagine

Imagine a Christmas tree with tinsel and lights,
Imagine singing carols on dark Christmas nights,
Imagine snow falling softly on the ground,
Imagine Christmas music heard all around,
Imagine decorations hung in every room,
Imagine hearing music and happy Christmas tunes,
Imagine hot chocolate in front of the fire,
Imagine presents stacked higher and higher.
Now imagine you're homeless on a cold winter night.
With no warmth and no Christmas lights.
Imagine and know how lucky you are
To have a home, a family and the best Christmas by far.

Joe Peters (13)
The Thetford Academy, Thetford

Imagine

Sometimes I think about
what's going to happen?
When we're not going to be here anymore,
I always imagine
that we're going to live again
Like a human or an animal
Have a new life
And that we are going to live forever
But then everything can be way more complicated than I think.
There are so many theories
about the afterlife,
but no one knows
what will actually happen.
There are so many things that we don't know about life,
Like where are we going to be at the end,
Here?
Or we not going to exist anymore?

Evita Rasplochaite (14)
The Thetford Academy, Thetford

Sun

She is perfect
Ever so perfect
Her beauty and intelligence proportioned
Her warmth and comfort pre-eminent
She is the sun
She is the Andromeda
Imagination is the closest I can be to her
Imagination is the closest I can be to being noticed by her
Yet
No matter how much I wish
No matter how much I visualise
No matter how much I imagine
She will always be the sun
She will always be the Andromeda
And I will always be
Me
A quark
Something so tiny and invisible to the human eye
Something she won't notice.

Jaydie-Ann Lamb (13)
The Thetford Academy, Thetford

If Only I Was Her

There was this girl in my school
She had a perfect body, dusty blonde hair,
Eyes as blue as the Atlantic.
She knew how to make you laugh
She knew everyone liked her
She was humble about it
Her parents were a perfect loving couple
How could she not turn out perfect?
She was a talented, pretty girl
With so many friends.
I have brown hair, blue eyes
An unperfect body that hides away in a hoody all year long,
I can make you laugh but not a lot,
Not many people like me.
My parents weren't perfect.
If only I was her...

Vanesa Berzina (12)
The Thetford Academy, Thetford

Grandad In Heaven

Although you sleep in Heaven now,
You're not that far away,
My heart is full of memories
And you're with me every day,
You lived your life with meaning
And with a grin upon your face,
A world that was full of happiness
Is now an empty place,
People say that only time
Will heal a broken heart
But just like with me and you,
Grandad, it has been torn apart
I know you are at peace now
And in a place where you are free,
But I imagine that you will meet me
At the golden gates
When Heaven calls for me.

Kayla Bogacki (14)
The Thetford Academy, Thetford

Imagine If You Had Superpowers

Imagine you could be invisible, invincible
Just don't be despicable.
Imagine if you could see people through walls
And see them run through halls.
Imagine if you could fly
Oh so high.
Imagine if you could teleport
Don't deny it.
Imagine if you could read people's minds
But yours and mine.
Imagine if you couldn't hear the movement of people moving
But why?
Imagine if you could change the weather
But no one else could do so.
Imagine you actually had superpowers
Oh so incredible.

Lucy Ellis (11)
The Thetford Academy, Thetford

Just Imagine If...

Imagine if homework wasn't a thing.
Imagine if humans never existed.
Imagine if climate change never existed.
Imagine, just imagine...

Imagine if there was no law.
Imagine if you stayed a kid forever.
Imagine if dinosaurs lived.
Imagine if you could share brains.
Imagine, just imagine...

Imagine if you lived in a dream.
Imagine if everything was for free.
Imagine if you could live forever.
Imagine if genies were real.
Imagine if nothing could go extinct.
Imagine, just imagine...

Dylan Odey (14)
The Thetford Academy, Thetford

Imagine If

Imagine if time travel was real
And you could go to any time period whenever you wanted,
Imagine if magic was real
And you could really make people disappear.

Imagine if aliens were real
And they were actually green and stubby,
Imagine if we all had unlimited money
And everybody could buy whatever they wanted.

Imagine if everybody got along
And bullying didn't exist,
Imagine if everyone was equal
And how much easier that would make some people's lives.

Imagine if...

Faith Pleszko (14)
The Thetford Academy, Thetford

Imagine

Imagine if we were the size of giants,
Imagine if we were friends with ghosts,
Imagine if we all had the same everything.

Imagine if we were able to learn anything,
Imagine if we were able to walk on air,
Imagine if we were as tall as trees.

Imagine if we were as tiny as mice,
Imagine if we were as cold as ice,
Imagine if we were all alone.

Imagine if our imagination was real,
Imagine if our imagination had personality,
Imagine if we didn't have imagination at all.

Sarah Soares (13)
The Thetford Academy, Thetford

Imagine

Imagine waking up to forests on fire,
Land disappearing with the sea levels getting higher.
Imagine a world without plastic,
Now isn't that drastic?
Imagine a world without animals,
War and conflict happening in the capitals.
Imagine the ozone layer disappearing,
Urban decay is nearing.
Imagine the temperature rising,
Icebergs downsizing.
Imagine deforestation,
Pollution in operation.
Imagine COVID killing the population,
That's a bad situation.

Sophie Clarke (14)
The Thetford Academy, Thetford

Imagine Being Able To Fly

Imagine, imagine being able to fly,
Imagine being able to soar through the sky,
Soaring as high as the birds could fly,
Oh, I always wish I could fly,
I wish I could fly as high as the clouds,
Watching the birds fly around.

Imagine, imagine being able to fly,
Oh, I would love to soar that high,
As high as the birds and as high as the clouds,
Watching them always flying around,
Oh, I will always dream of flying around,
Imagine, imagine being able to fly…

Lily-Mai Brady (12)
The Thetford Academy, Thetford

Imagine No Fear

Can you imagine a world with no fear
And everything you dreamed of would just then appear?
Imagine climbing the highest tall hill,
Without fear of falling, just enjoying the thrill

Imagine free-diving the deepest dark seas
And knowing for sure you'd be able to breathe,
Imagine exploring a deep enclosed cave
And the wonder, fascination and views you could save,
Imagine going after your wildest dreams,
You don't need to imagine, just to believe.

Tom Peters
The Thetford Academy, Thetford

Imagine If

Imagine if there was no pollution
Imagine if there were no bullies
Imagine if there were no haters
Imagine, oh imagine - imagine is all we can do.

Imagine if wolves were human
Imagine if sheep were human
Imagine if cats were human
Imagine, oh imagine - imagine is all we can do.

Imagine if there was no homework
Imagine if there were no detentions
Imagine if there was no work
Imagine, oh imagine - imagine is all we can do.

Amber Way (12)
The Thetford Academy, Thetford

If I Was Anime

I would imagine being anime
F lying across the sky

I 'm a huge anime fan

W anting to travel the world
A lways being cute
S ometimes sad, sometimes happy

A nime is great
N ever watch inappropriate anime
I f anime isn't your thing, then watch Pokémon
M aybe My Hero Academia sometimes. Always smiling
E ven though it's a dream, I like it.

Brontë Manning (12)
The Thetford Academy, Thetford

Imagine

I magine yourself in a world of your own,
M ake yourself feel safe,
A llow yourself to be free,
G ive in to all your fantasies,
I nclude all the things that make you happy,
N arrate your own life for once.
E uphoria, that's what you feel, until you hear the sound of your friends calling your name.

You look at the time and the lesson is over already.
You now have to enter the real world again!

Rugile Slanciauskaite
The Thetford Academy, Thetford

Imagination Is Everything

Imagine a world where everything is true,
As true as it can be.
Imagine a world where everything stays the same,
But you wanna change it somehow.
Imagine a world where the people you love are all gone,
Just like that.
Imagine a world where you no longer exist,
But only one person remembers you.

If you imagine,
You can create anything.
When you can create anything,
You can imagine,
Because imagination is everything.

Jasmine Reyes (12)
The Thetford Academy, Thetford

Just Imagine

What would you do if aliens took over?
Imagine if your best friend was a king
What would you do?
Wouldn't it be lovely
Just imagine what you could do
Imagine if someone betrayed you.
What would you do if aliens took over?
Just imagine, what would you do?
Oh, wouldn't it be cool!
What would you do?
Wouldn't it feel cool?
Wouldn't it be scary?
As you feel the betrayal in your veins
What would you do?

Patrick Chaves (11)
The Thetford Academy, Thetford

Underwater

Imagine if the world was upside down.
What if we all lived underwater and not in these little towns?
Imagine if we could swim and float around in the water,
Imagine seeing an octopus walking around with its daughter!
Imagine if girls were mermaids swimming around the sea,
Just sit and imagine how the world would be!
Would marine animals be like me?
Would they be able to see?
Imagine living underwater,
Oh, what a dream it would be.

Luciana Nuttel-Cid (12)
The Thetford Academy, Thetford

Imagine A World Without Music

M y life without music; I'll be honest, I'd absolutely lose it.
U sually, I'd sit there and think of what to do, but without it, I wouldn't have a clue.
S ometimes I get it wrong, but I know I'm right; if we didn't have music, we would die inside.
I love the fact that music is here, it makes us less moody and brings us some cheer.
C lap for all the musicians out there who make us laugh and cheer.

Lola Winstone (14)
The Thetford Academy, Thetford

A New Student

 A new student had arrived

 N ever knew about life
 E nded primary school a week ago
"W eak knowledge will never grow."

 S ometimes, he learned new things
 T urned around, trying to get names
 U nicycle he rode all day
 D ad at work all day
 E ach morning, he went to school
 N ever wanting to project his voice
 T oday he starts being brave.

Aleksander Nowicki (11)
The Thetford Academy, Thetford

Imagine If You Were

Imagine if you were flying in the sky
Imagine if you couldn't tell a lie
Imagine if you were rich
Imagine if a ride you were able to hitch
Imagine if you couldn't say hi
Imagine if you could just try
Imagine if you were swimming
Imagine if from your favourite superstar you just got a ring
Imagine you could be known
Or even heir to the throne
Just imagine you were, you could try.

Just imagine.

Aaron Harvey (11)
The Thetford Academy, Thetford

Invisibility

I magine you can't be seen
N ever being caught
V isualise the opportunities
I nternational concealed traveller
S uperhero superpower
I mpossibilities are endless
B oundaries don't exist any more
I nstead, you can be free
L ike a bird, you can roam
I nconspicuous, the disguise
T ravelling to the undiscovered
Y ou hold the key.

Alfie Pittman (11)
The Thetford Academy, Thetford

Imagine...

I magination is where dreams are made and goals are set.
M indset is the tool, don't have any regret.
A mountain must be climbed.
G et some rest, you're not being timed.
I won't be distracted from getting my result.
N o words will distract me, I won't listen to any insults.
E veryone needs imagination, it's where happiness begins. Stay on track and everyone wins.

Nevaeh Azevedo (11)
The Thetford Academy, Thetford

Imagine If You

Imagine if you cracked the scales paradigm
And you controlled the building blocks of the universe
Imagine if your dreams were real
And you could shape reality.
Imagine if you were immortal
You could live to, let's say, the year 5000 trillion!
Imagine if you and everyone you knew were just a reality simulator
And were just game avatars.
Imagine if you could see what everyone was thinking
Just imagine.

Dylan Higgins Fitzpatrick (11)
The Thetford Academy, Thetford

If I Were A Toy

If I were a toy, yes, a toy!
I would belong to a boy, a nice boy
What toy would I be?
You ask!
I would be colourful and bright
To make everything right
Give happiness and joy
To the little boy
I am a toy - what toy?
I am a car - a wonderful car
Plenty of fun
For everyone
Hours and hours
Pass on by
Lots of fun
For everyone
Car in the garage
Time to rest.

Fergus Steward (14)
The Thetford Academy, Thetford

Imagine If We Were All Equal

Imagine if we were all equal
If everything was peaceful

You couldn't speak for yourself,
You wouldn't have to seek for friends.

There would be no need to be exploring,
Life would be so boring.

If we were all the same
You would not need to learn a name
You couldn't claim
Your own prize.

I am happy we are all different
It makes life magnificent.

Mia Macpherson-Youldon (11)
The Thetford Academy, Thetford

If They Knew The Real Me

If people knew the real me,
They would know I'm different.

If people knew the real me,
They would support me more.

If people knew the real me,
They would understand why I'm alone.
They would know I have autism.

If people knew the real me,
They would know how hard it is to voice I have autism
So I would need help
In this invisible war called COVID-19.

Lilly-Ann O'Connor (11)
The Thetford Academy, Thetford

Imagine

Imagine if animals could talk
Imagine if toys came to life
Imagine if you could walk on the edge of the world
Imagine if you could fly
Imagine if you could get everything for free
Imagine if kids controlled adults
Imagine if the world ended
Imagine there was another life after you die
Imagine if everyone couldn't talk
Imagine if you were the last person on Earth.

Tianna Jade Mark-Conlon (12)
The Thetford Academy, Thetford

Imagine

Imagine if you could see what people were thinking
Oh, the power you would have
The power to hurt
Or even the power to torture
It would be an evil power
Or it would be a power to bring people together
Love and harmony between people
Or even just using it for a laugh.
Sounds nice, doesn't it?
Well, too bad it can't happen
But you can still imagine.

Thomas Norkett (12)
The Thetford Academy, Thetford

Invisibility

You might dream of being invisible,
When actually, it's quite miserable,
It fills me with tears
Although there are no fears.

Without anyone noticing,
Without anyone knowing
Where I'm going,
Or where I have been travelling.

Unless my voice is heard,
Or my footprints seen,
I am just like a shadow,
Of the person I once had been.

Daniel Bailey-Green (12)
The Thetford Academy, Thetford

One Wish

I wish I had some time with you
To fly amongst the pigeons
And tell you funny stories
About how my life has been living.
I wish we could go back
To when you poured your favourite juice,
I would pretend I enjoyed it
When, secretly, I despised it.
So, fly high, Grandad,
You really must know,
There wouldn't be a moment
Where I would let you go.

Chloe Bowley (11)
The Thetford Academy, Thetford

Imagine

Imagine if your wings never flew.
Imagine if the wind never blew.
Imagine always being in the sky.
Imagine always being so high.
Imagine being all alone.
Imagine never having a home.
Imagine flying over the sea.
Imagine being so free.
Imagine never being the runner.
Imagine always being the hunter.
Imagine no people.
Imagine being an eagle.

Keira-Marie Mulligan (13)
The Thetford Academy, Thetford

Imagine

Imagine if we were all hand in hand
Imagine if everyone was happy
Everyone less snappy.

Imagine never feeling sad
Imagine if the world was bad
Imagine never finding a warning
Imagine no global warming
Imagine never feeling love
Imagine no feeling of crying
Imagine no loved ones dying.

Imagine no COVID-19

Just imagine.

Molly Sawbridge (12)
The Thetford Academy, Thetford

Imagine

Imagine you could beat the war,
Imagine you could be immortal,
Just imagine your dreams were reality
And wishes came true,
Imagine,
Just imagine,
If life was easy,
There would be no point,
If everything you learned was easy,
You would have no failures to learn from,
So, although life is tough, just imagine,
Just believe
In yourself!

Jaiden Lowry (11)
The Thetford Academy, Thetford

Imagine If Humans Were Extinct

Imagine if humans were extinct
Grass could grow long and tall,
Animals could roam,
Look!
A deer in a skyscraper
But not sorting out paper, no,
Because now they rule the world
No more plastic because they have learned.
The animals in the zoo no longer in a cage, no,
They can live free until old age,
So imagine if humans were extinct.

Sophie Cunningham (12)
The Thetford Academy, Thetford

Imagine If...

Imagine a world
With no Holocaust.
Imagine a world
Where nobody cries.
Imagine,
Imagine
The strength of
The world's love.

Imagine a world
Where all love is strong.

Imagine if you won the lottery,
You could buy your dreams.

Imagine if you had one wish,
That wish would come true.

Elena-Miruna Mincu (14)
The Thetford Academy, Thetford

Imagine If Murder Was Legal

The town would be plastered in red,
Many people would end up dead,
Imagine that, stepping over heads
As lifeless eyes jealously watch your life,
Whilst you carry your favourite knife.
You plan your next life to take
As people suddenly awake.
A reality check was all they needed,
That your own demise was what they pleaded.

Nikodem Olszewski (13)
The Thetford Academy, Thetford

Imagine

Imagine if there were no punishments
Many crimes being committed and no one saving humanity
Anyone volunteering to restore normality?
The world in danger
The world destroyed
People too scared to leave their safety zone
Glass all over the street from where banks were robbed
Someone needs to save us because this is wrong.

Natalie Daly (12)
The Thetford Academy, Thetford

2020

It's like a big fire
COVID isn't a liar

We have all lost our families and friends
Will it ever end?

I feel like I am going to cry
Because some people have died

What did we do?
I have no clue

Some people's lives are ending
And that's who we're remembering.

Rosie Higgins (11)
The Thetford Academy, Thetford

Just Imagine

Just imagine a bolt of lightning hitting a tree.
Imagine a storm remaining all morning and all night.
Imagine dawn rising.
Earth awakening.
Flowers rising.
Birds tweeting.
Imagine the world was calm and clear.
The sun yellow like lions' fur
And then the moonlight showing its shimmers.
Just imagine.

Grace Cuff (11)
The Thetford Academy, Thetford

Moon, World And Life

Imagine if the world was falling apart
Or if the moon had a heart.
Imagine if you were alone on Earth
Or if your best friend died whilst giving birth.
Imagine if all of your friends were gone
If they never sang a song.
I don't have to imagine any of that
Because it is my life and that is a fact.

Grace Palmer (12)
The Thetford Academy, Thetford

Imagine If

Imagine if Coronavirus wasn't a thing.
Imagine if everyone were robots.
Imagine if everyone knew nothing.
Imagine if everyone was rich.
Imagine if everyone was fake.
Imagine if there was no king or queen.
Imagine if there were no animals in the world.
Imagine if everyone were family.

Summer Finmager (11)
The Thetford Academy, Thetford

Just Imagine

Can you imagine being able to see your loved ones who have passed away
If Heaven had visiting hours
And being able to say, "I love you,"
To their face?
Just imagine that you could give them a call
And they would answer
And you tell them about your day.

Just imagine.

TJ Curtis (14)
The Thetford Academy, Thetford

Difference

Imagine you could change one thing
What would you change?
Imagine you could say one thing
What would you say?
Imagine you could do one thing
What would you do?
Imagine you could be one thing
What would you be?
Now ask the person next to you.
Their answer will be different.

Kia Dodds (14)
The Thetford Academy, Thetford

Imagine

Just imagine:

- **I** ndex fingers as pinkies,
- **M** edia not existing,
- **A** ffording a whole country's price so you could buy it,
- **G** alaxies were all discovered,
- **I** ce cream did not exist,
- **N** o one would survive COVID-19,
- **E** ngland in communism.

Jakub Kosciewicz
The Thetford Academy, Thetford

Imagine

Imagine if your lifespan was infinite,
All the things you could do,
The things you could learn,
You'd be like a kid in a candy store.
But the things that entail
Living forever
Could lead to such boredom,
You'd wish you'd never wanted
A life that lonely anyway.

Mason Edmunds (13)
The Thetford Academy, Thetford

Imagine

Imagine eating but not drinking,
Working but not sleeping,
Imagine the world as wonders
Weird but meaningful,
Imagining makes us feel...
Thoughtful
And thoughtful we shall be,
Our minds are the same,
They work but think differently.
Be different...

Clive Killick (14)
The Thetford Academy, Thetford

Imagine

I magine if you were immortal
M agic comes from within
A nything would be possible
G ather thousands of friends
I would be a different person
N othing would be the same
E verlasting, for eternity...

Freddie Griffiths (12)
The Thetford Academy, Thetford

Imagine I Were Her

Imagine I were her
Imagine I were perfect
The perfect brown hair that flows when the wind picks up
The perfect hazel eyes
The perfect face
The perfect everything
Imagine I were her
That's all I can do...
Imagine.

Lilly Macro (13)
The Thetford Academy, Thetford

Imagine

- **I** magine we survived,
- **M** anmade monsters defeated,
- **A** ll is safe and all is
- **G** uarded, everyone cheers,
- **I** n the night, they celebrate a
- **N** ever-ending party, creating
- **E** verlasting peace.

Alfie Dale (13)
The Thetford Academy, Thetford

Imagine

Imagine if everyone I hated
Left the world for a day -
How perfect would the world be?
Or would I have no games to play?
If everyone I hated
Left the world for a day,
Only I would be happy
And my smile would fade away.

Elise Conway (13)
The Thetford Academy, Thetford

Imagine

Imagine a pig
With a big purple wig
Imagine a car
In the shape of a star
Imagine a bear
Wearing pink underwear
Imagine a fox
Wearing big blue socks
Imagine if you
Had the skin colour blue
Just imagine!

Samuel Teixeira (12)
The Thetford Academy, Thetford

Imagine If Everyone Was Equal

- **E** veryone could never be equal, not even twins.
- **Q** uantity doesn't matter.
- **U** nited together as one.
- **A** ll together as one, you all matter.
- **L** ove is all around, together forever, include everyone.

Megan James (11)
The Thetford Academy, Thetford

YOUNG WRITERS INFORMATION

We hope you have enjoyed reading this book – and that you will continue to in the coming years.

If you're a young writer who enjoys reading and creative writing, or the parent of an enthusiastic poet or story writer, do visit our website www.youngwriters.co.uk. Here you will find free competitions, workshops and games, as well as recommended reads, a poetry glossary and our blog. There's lots to keep budding writers motivated to write!

If you would like to order further copies of this book, or any of our other titles, then please give us a call or order via your online account.

Young Writers
Remus House
Coltsfoot Drive
Peterborough
PE2 9BF
(01733) 890066
info@youngwriters.co.uk

Join in the conversation!
Tips, news, giveaways and much more!

YoungWritersUK @YoungWritersCW @YoungWritersCW